Bob's White Christmas

Adapted by
Alison Inches

Based on the script by
Jimmy Hibbert

Illustrated by
Mel Grant

Simon Spotlight

New York   London   Toronto   Sydney   Singapore

Dizzy twirled and clapped her front tires together. "It's Christmas Eve!" she cried. "We're going to have loads of fun!"

"That's right, Dizzy," said Bob as he carried a large box from his workshop. "It's time to decorate the yard for the holidays!"

"Here comes the Christmas tree!" called Wendy,
as Scoop lowered the tree into the middle of the yard.
"Hooray!" cheered the machines.

"What a wonderful tree!" exclaimed Bob,
pulling a string of Christmas lights from the box.
"**Can we trim it?**" said Bob
"**Yes, we can!**" yelled the machines.

As they worked, Dizzy noticed a snowflake—then another one, and then another one. "Look!" she exclaimed. "We're going to have a white Christmas!"

"I have an idea. Let's build a snowman with all of this new snow," suggested Bob.

Everyone pitched in. Scoop gathered snow, Lofty lowered a traffic cone onto the snowman's head, and Bob gave it a bolt nose.

"A snowman fit for a builder!" Bob said proudly.

Just then Wendy hurried into the yard. "Farmer Pickles needs your help, Bob," she said. "He's snowed in and needs you to dig him out."

"Come on, Scoop," said Bob. "This is a job for your snowplow." Bob snapped the plow into place and climbed aboard Scoop.
"Can we plow it?" said Bob.
"Yes, we can!" yelled Scoop.

After they left, Wendy found Bob's cell phone under the tree.
"Oh, dear!" she cried. "Bob's forgotten his cell phone.
Dizzy, will you take it to him?"
"No problem," answered Dizzy.
So Wendy tucked the cell phone safely inside Dizzy's mixer.

As Dizzy rolled along, the snow gathered on top of her.
"B-B-Brrr!" she said, shivering. "It's really cold out here!
I'd better take a shortcut."
She zoomed through the open gate.

Meanwhile, across a field, Spud slid down a snowy hill. "Whee! Whoo-hoo! Look out!" he yelled. "Here comes Spud the super slippery scarecrow!"

Bonkity bonk! Thud! Spud crashed into a shivering pile of snow. "Help!" cried Spud, running for the farmhouse. "It's a snow monster!"

Bob and Scoop had just finished plowing Farmer Pickles's driveway when Spud came running over.

"What's the matter, Spud?" asked Farmer Pickles.

"I just saw a snow monster!" cried Spud. "It's huge! And scary!"

"Hmmm," said Bob. "We'd better go have a look!"

When they got to the field, Spud pointed to the snow monster.
"That's not a snow monster," said Bob. "That's just Dizzy
covered in snow! What happened, Dizzy?"
"You f–f–forgot your cell phone," said Dizzy, shivering. "I tried
to bring it to you, but I got st–st–stuck in the snow."
"Poor thing! Let's get you home!" said Bob.

Back at home, Bob remembered that he had promised Mrs. Percival he would play Santa Claus and deliver presents to her schoolchildren on Christmas Eve. He quickly put on his Santa suit. "Ho! Ho! Ho!" said Bob, admiring himself in the mirror.

Outside, Wendy had dressed Muck to look like a sleigh and Dizzy to look like a reindeer.

"You look great, Muck!" said Bob.

"My goodness," Bob said, turning to Dizzy. "A reindeer *and* a snow monster all in one day!"

Then off they went up and over the hill to the schoolhouse.

Mrs. Percival's schoolchildren loved Bob's presents. "Thank you for the gifts, Bob!" said Mrs. Percival.

"It's been our pleasure," said Bob. Then he shook Muck's reins, and they headed for home.
And very soon after that, Christmas Eve turned into . . .

Christmas Day!
Santa Claus had come during the night and left presents for everyone.
"I love ripping the paper!" said Muck.
"Look what I got!" yelled Roley.
"This is just what I've always wanted!" exclaimed Scoop.
"Yippee!" cried Dizzy.